This Book Belongs To:

_____

Published and distributed by

Elf-Garb, LLC
P.O. Box 366, Weymouth, MA 02188
info@elf-garb.com
www.elf-garb.com

ELF~GARB

For information on how to order bulk copies of this book
or other Elf-Garb products, please send an email to sales@elf-garb.com.

This book has been illustrated by Jeff Beckman
Based on the character design of Diego Aguirre

Layout by Robin Wrighton

Amos the Elf and his Magical Pajamas / Kelley A. Joyce

Library of Congress Control Number: 2012909036

ISBN-13: 978-0-9881822-3-3

Second Edition - 1st Printing
June 2013

Printed in the United States

To
Emma ♥

2015

Amos the Elf
and his Magical Pajamas

by Kelley A. Joyce

Illustrated by Jeff Beckman & Character design by Diego Aguirre

Warmly Yours

Kelley Joyce

Dedication

This book is dedicated to my husband and
two sons, Johnny and Kurt, who gave me the
courage and support to become an author of a
children's book. This story is based upon our families'
long-standing annual tradition of receiving Amos' magical
Elf Pajamas on the eve of every Christmas.

I would like to express my gratitude to the many people who
helped me bring Amos to life. Deborah Thomas Drew, ever the
optimist, introduced me to the illustrators of this book, Jeff Beckman
and Diego Aquirre, whose illustrations, talent and craft brought Amos
from my imagination to the pages of this book. Darlene Adams, an accomplished
author, gave me the courage and inspiration to begin this project. Bob Keezer's superb
genius brought Amos from paper to plush doll. Colette Bythrow provided unending support
and reassurance every day, and her son Billy was a model for little Amos. Robin Wrighton, who
shared ideas and brought magic to the design.

Joyfully yours,
Kelley A. Joyce

Meet the Tucks

Edward

Eloise

Amos

This story is about
an adorable and captivating
five-year-old orphaned elf named
A - M - O - S (A Merry Ole Soul). Amos grows
up and fulfills his dream of sharing his family
tradition with others by delivering magical Elf Pajamas.
As you read along, you will discover how the spirit of the holiday
season brings magic
to all who believe.

Amos Edward Tuck was an orphaned elf...

...whose one wish was to be adopted by an adoring family.

When Amos was five, Edward and Eloise adopted the little elf. They took him home to live with them in the forests of the North Pole.

Amos loved spending time with his father who was a gifted builder. They worked together in his workshop drawing up plans and building toys for the holiday season.

Amos' mother was a talented seamstress. Sometimes Amos would help his mother as she sewed clothes for the children in a nearby orphanage.

5

On the days before Christmas, Amos and his friends had a hard time paying attention in school as they waited for all the excitement, joy and fun of the holiday to begin.

After school, Amos and his friends would venture outdoors
into the wilderness to play with all the little critters in the forest.

On the eve of Christmas, Amos would sit by the fire with his parents, eagerly awaiting the spirit of Christmas to arrive.
In Amos' mind, time did not pass quickly enough.

Just as Amos began to fall asleep, he heard the faint sound of chimes outside
the cabin door. He looked to his mother with curiosity. She leaned over and
whispered to him, "Look outside the door."

Amos looked outside his door and much to his surprise, there beneath the star-filled
sky, he found a fancy wrapped gift box. Amos took the box inside to show his parents.

Excitedly, he opened the box and to his delight found a pair of brightly colored pajamas. As he lifted the pajamas out of the box, tiny twinkling stars danced around them and he exclaimed, "Wow, they must be magical Elf Pajamas!"

Amos was eager to see what would happen when he wore his new magical Elf Pajamas to
bed. He quickly ran upstairs to his room, slipped them on and climbed under the covers.

"Good night, Mama," Amos said. "Good night, Papa."
Feeling warm and cozy, Amos snuggled up under the soft covers of his bed where
he could feel the magic of his new Elf Pajamas beginning to work. His imagination was
filled with the Christmas spirit as he nodded off to sleep.

5 Year Old Amos

10 Year Old Amos

15 Year Old Amos

Amos Today

Year after year as Amos grew, a new pair of magical Elf Pajamas would arrive each Christmas Eve on his doorstep, bringing joy and Christmas spirit to his heart.

To this day, Amos works to fulfill his dream of sharing his family tradition.
Every Christmas Eve he ventures out on his sled to deliver magical Elf Pajamas
to all the boys and girls who believe!

15

The End

Amos'
Magical Activity
Book

Coloring Pages * Mazes * Puzzles & More

CAN YOU DRAW A LINE TO MATCH THE PAJAMA TOPS TO THE MATCHING PAJAMA BOTTOMS?

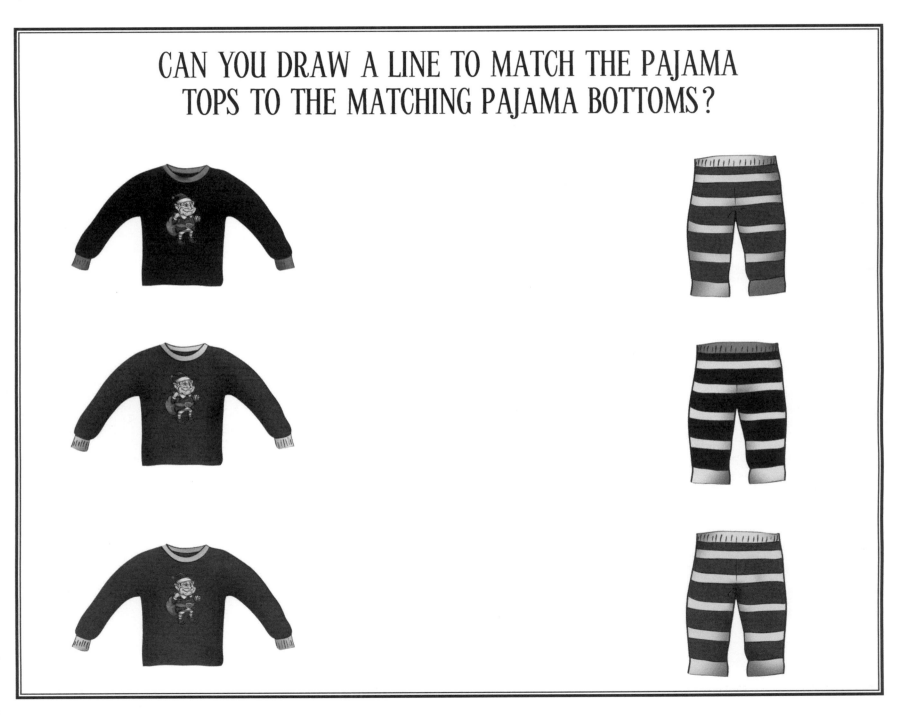

FOLLOW THE NUMBERS TO CONNECT THE DOTS TO DISCOVER WHAT AMOS BROUGHT?

COLOR LITTLE AMOS

Where does Amos live?

A.   North Pole

B.   South Pole

C.   Alaska

What does Amos find outside
his cabin door?

A.   Gift Box

B.   Moose

C.   Rocking Chair

COLOR MR. TUCK

What is Mr. Tuck's job?

A.   Doctor

B.   Builder

C.   Policeman

What is Mr. Tuck's first name?

A.   Connor

B.   Edward

C.   Billy

COLOR MRS. TUCK

What is Mrs. Tuck's talent?

A.   Dance

B.   Singer

C.   Seamstress

What is Mrs. Tuck's first name?

A.   Ella

B.   Elizabeth

C.   Eloise

COLOR AMOS

What does Amos deliver
on Christmas Eve?

A.   Cookies

B.   Pajamas

C.   Mail

What does Amos carry on his back?

A.   Sack

B.   Sled

C.   Back Pack

CAN YOU SPOT THE DIFFERENCES
BETWEEN AMOS 1 AND AMOS 2

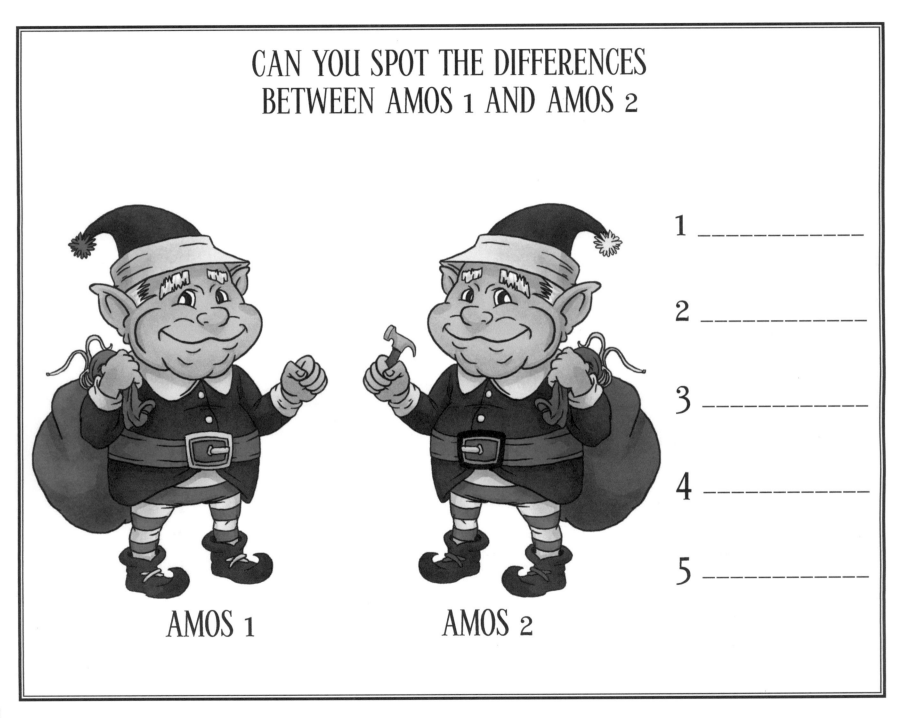

AMOS 1

AMOS 2

1 _____

2 _____

3 _____

4 _____

5 _____

CAN YOU DRAW A LINE THROUGH THE MAZE TO HELP AMOS FIND HIS MAGICAL PAJAMAS?

FINISH

START

HELP AMOS SOLVE THE CROSSWORD PUZZLE

ACROSS

2   What Amos delivers on Christmas Eve

5   What presents may come in

6   Mr. Tuck's job

7   What Amos heard outside the cabin door

8   Where Amos goes to learn

DOWN

1   What Amos' special pajamas are

3   Where Amos and his friends like to play

4   What Amos Edward Tuck was in the beginning

HELP AMOS FIND THE HIDDEN WORDS

AMOS

CHRISTMAS

DREAM

ELF

GIFT

HOLIDAY

PAJAMAS

SEASON

TRADITION

WISH

```
Y  T  P  S  T  C  J  M  E
M  F  A  W  J  H  V  S  L
E  I  J  I  H  R  J  E  Z
L  G  A  S  O  I  U  A  L
F  D  M  H  L  S  H  S  A
T  R  A  D  I  T  I  O  N
Z  E  S  S  D  M  M  N  E
H  A  D  G  A  A  M  O  S
J  M  T  K  Y  S  D  U  W
```

Answers

Page 20 Where does Amos live?
A. North Pole

What does Amos find outside his cabin door?
A. Gift Box

Page 21 What is Mr. Tuck's job?
B. Builder

What is Mr. Tuck's first name?
B. Edward

Page 22 What is Mrs. Tuck's talent?
C. Seamstress

What is Mrs. Tuck's first name?
C. Eloise

Page 23 What does Amos deliver on Christmas Eve?
B. Pajamas

What does Amos carry on his back?
A. Sack

Page 24 - Did You Spot All the Differences?

1. Yellow pom-pom on his hat

2. Red bag on his shoulder

3. Hammer in his hand

4. Black trim on his belt buckle

5. Pink shoe laces

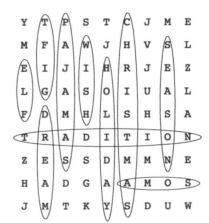

Crossword Puzzle Answer
Page 26

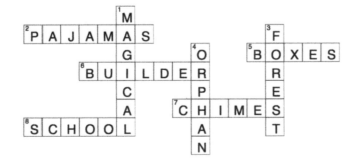

Word Search Puzzle Answer
Page 27

Here is a space to write about something special
you want to remember from this holiday season!

My Magical Memories